**Praise for Mal Peet and *The Family Tree***

"Likely to be the best children's book you will read this year ... Peet is a profound storyteller" *THE TIMES*

"Mal Peet wrote with extraordinary sensitivity and insight and this novella is testimony to his talent" *ANDREA REECE*

"I love this wonderful book. How does Mal Peet do so much in such a short space? It's engrossing, haunting, beautifully written" *DAVID ALMOND*

"A timely reminder of what a magician Mal Peet was. How you cast such a powerful, intoxicating spell with so few words is beyond me" *PHIL EARLE*

"For thoughtful, intelligent young readers, no writer of this century writes better than Mal Peet" *MEG ROSOFF*

"A story of such challenging emotional complexity, yet told so simply, so gently. No wonder Mal Peet is a story-teller we miss so much" *KEITH GRAY*

"Rarely does one come across a children's tale written quite so hauntingly, leaving one drained and emotional but also strangely hopeful, nostalgic and understanding of human nature, and in particular fatherhood" *MINERVAREADS.COM*

# GOOD
# BOY

First published in 2019 in Great Britain by
Barrington Stoke Ltd
18 Walker Street, Edinburgh, EH3 7LP

www.barringtonstoke.co.uk

A CIP catalogue record for this book is available
from the British Library upon request

ISBN: 978-1-78112-852-7

Printed in China by Leo

# GOOD BOY

### MAL PEET

Illustrations by

### EMMA SHOARD

Barrington Stoke

*For Barrington Moy*

# 1

You are walking down the garden path.  You
are wearing strange and heavy clothes.  Your
hands explore them but do not recognise them.

# GOOD BOY

*It's very dark, but your feet know the way. The gate opens without you touching it. You walk through it, but then you are not where you ought to be, on the street where the parked cars wait calmly for the morning. No, you are in a wild and limitless space. The wind's moan swells, fades, swells again. You walk on, but then your clever feet refuse to move because you are at the edge of a precipice. You don't want to look down, but you can't help yourself. So you do look down, and at the bottom of the black and measureless drop there are bright wriggling worms, yellow and white and red.*

*Because they make you feel dizzy and sick, you lift your eyes away from them. You turn back the way you've come, but the garden and the house have gone. All you can see is the ragged horizon where the pitch-dark of the land meets the dark grey of the sky.*

*You understand that you're waiting for something.*

# GOOD BOY

*And here it comes. Walking along the horizon. At first it's just a ripple, like something behind a curtain. Then the moon opens its eye and you can see that the thing walks on all fours with its head lowered. It's a dog, a very large dog, and although you have never been afraid of dogs, this one fills you with terror. It's as though you are drowning in*

fear; it's as though fear has filled you up right to the top of your throat and you have only one last breath to scream with.

So you scream.

The dog hears you and turns its head, its ears twitching. Then it disappears, its black shape lost in the surrounding blackness. But you know it's coming towards you, and there's nothing you can do except stand there with your back to the abyss and wait while your last scream echoes and echoes and echoes.

**2**

Then there is light and warm arms and a voice.

"Hey. Hey, Sandie. Sandie? It's all right.
Shush. It's all right. It's all right, sweetie.
God, you frightened the life out of me with all
that screaming."

The biscuity smell of her mother's
bed-warmth.

But still the dog coming at her out of the
night.

Then the bedside light making everything shockingly normal.

Gone.

"You were having a bad dream, babe. That's all. It's OK."

The child's heart beats against her ribs as if it were trying to escape its cage.

"Can I sleep with you, Mum?"

"Sure. Come on."

In the big bed she snugs herself against her mother's body.

"Wanna tell me about the dream, Sandie?"

"It was about a big bad dog."

"We all have those, sweetie," her mother murmurs. "It's normal. Don't worry about it. It's OK."

## 3

But it isn't OK, and it isn't normal. The dog

continues to haunt Sandie Callan's sleep. Often

it is just a dark flicker that passes through her

dreams like a shadow along a wall. A glimpse

of a black muscular shape patrolling the edge

of a gloomy sky or turning to look at her. Then

gone. At such times, Sandie's breathing will

stumble, or she will groan, then sleep on, more

or less peacefully. At other times, it's the

full nightmare: the terrible drop at her feet,
the dog getting invisibly closer, then its eyes,
blank mirrors of moonlight, emerging from
the darkness, closer – much closer! – than she'd
expected. Its harsh and eager breathing. Then
the screaming starts, and Sandie wakes into a
room full of screams.

Sometimes months pass before the great
black dog comes in the night. But Sandie
always knows it will return. She grows to fear
sleep. She fights sleep off. But sleep is a crafty
enemy and starts to sneak up on her during
the daytime.

**4**

When Sandie is ten years old, her head teacher

invites her mother to come to the school

to discuss the "problem". A visit to a child

psychiatrist is arranged.

The psychiatrist is a softly spoken woman

who wears spectacular earrings, which Sandie

envies. Her name is Aziza.

# GOOD BOY

Gently, she teases the details of Sandie's nightmare out of her.  After their third session, she asks to speak to Sandie's mother alone.

"The truth is," Aziza says, "that we have very little idea about what causes recurring nightmares unless they are about something that has actually happened to the person having them.  Sandie tells me that she has never been attacked by a dog or anything else. Is that true?"

"Yes.  As far as I know."

Aziza thinks about that answer.

Then she says, "I'm sorry, Mrs Callan, but I need to ask you this. You are a single parent, is that correct? And you have a part-time job in the post office?"

"Yes. So what?"

"So, well, I'm sorry, as I say, but ..."

Jenny Callan says stiffly, "Sandie is never left alone. I don't bring men to our house. She's never been abused in any way. Is that what you were asking?"

A tense moment like an intruder in the room.

Then Aziza says, "OK. Thank you. So,

the other possible explanation for recurring

nightmares – the same nightmare – is that it's

a sort of habit. That even though it's weird and

frightening, it becomes normal. Familiar. That

people start to expect it. Even *want* it. Does

that make any sense to you?"

"Yes. I suppose so."

"So the trick is to break the habit somehow.

Look, this might seem a rather odd idea, but

have you ever thought about getting a dog? A

real dog, one that Sandie could care for?"

Jenny frowns. "What, like a sort of antidote?"

Aziza the psychiatrist leans back in her chair and says, "Yes, something like that. Is it worth a try, do you think?"

# 5

The puppy is a mongrel, his coat random

splashes of brown and white and black.  He

looks as though he'd got in the way of a team

of sloppy decorators.  His feet belong to a much

bigger dog, and he falls over them when Sandie

plays with him on the wee-flavoured rug.

"His mum's a spaniel," the woman who'd

put the advert in the paper tells them.  "I can't

honestly say what the father is.  Some sort of

terrier, at a guess.  There's one up the road

that might've done the dirty deed."

They take him home.

Sandie wants to call him Rabbit on account

of his long dangling ears, but her mother

thinks it would sound daft if they went on

walks and shouted "Here, Rabbit" at a dog.

So they settle on Rabbie.  He turns out to be

intelligent.  When he's spoken to, he has an

attentive way of tilting his head and sharply

focusing his eyes, those wet black buttons set

in his patchwork head.

Rabbie sleeps in a quilted cloth basket

under Sandie's bed.  Soon, and somehow, he

comes to know why.  When the terrible black

dog descends from the skyline of Sandie's

dreams, when she twists and groans, Rabbie emerges from under the bed with a warning resounding in his throat that swells into a bark.  Two of those do the trick.  Sandie slips free of the nightmare and reaches down to Rabbie, sleepily fondles the soft span of his skull between his ears.

"Good boy.  Good boy.  It's all right.  It's all right now.  Go back to sleep."

Gradually the gaps between the dream-dog's visits grow longer.  And when he does come, he keeps his distance, only watching her with his glittering eyes while

stalking by.

Then she'll hear Rabbie's warning rumble.

"Good boy." Her hand on his warm head.

"Good boy."

And eventually the beast vanishes from her

nights.

# 6

When Sandie Callan is eighteen, she goes away, to university. She is happy, most of the time, for the next three years. Rabbie misses her more than she misses him. When she comes home between university terms, he greets her with a mad dance, up on his back legs with his front paws dabbing at her. She takes him for walks but talks to her mobile, not to him.

\*

Sandie leaves university and wastes a year doing any old job for money. She doesn't come home very often. Then she decides, or discovers, what it is that she really wants to do. She fills in, very thoughtfully, an application form. It takes her two days. She goes for an interview, then another one.

She rings her mother.

"Mum? Mum, I did it! I passed the interview!"

"That's fantastic, sweetheart. I knew you would. Well done."

# GOOD BOY

There's something wrong with her mother's voice.

"Mum? Aren't you pleased?"

"Yes. Yes, of course I am. I'm very proud of you, darling."

It still isn't right, though.

"Mum? What's the matter?"

"It's just ... It's awful to have to tell you this today of all days, but ... well, Rabbie died this morning."

"Oh, no," Sandie says. "Oh my God. What happened? Was he ill? You never said anything."

"No. He was getting a bit blind, as you know. And he must've wandered into the road and got hit by a car or something. A neighbour found him. I know it's stupid, but I've been crying all day."

"Oh, Mum. I'm so sorry."

"It's all right. I really didn't want to spoil your day. It's ridiculous to get so upset over a dog."

\*

Later, Sandie makes other calls and goes to a pub to celebrate her new job with her friends. At one point, she gets tearful about her dog dying. Her mates tease her, and eventually she laughs about it. Then she goes back to her flat

and stumbles into bed.

# 7

*You are walking down the garden path. You are wearing—*

No.

*You are not where you ought to be, on the street where the parked cars wait—*

No. Please, no.

*It appears on the horizon. It's just a shape at first, like a ripple behind a curtain—*

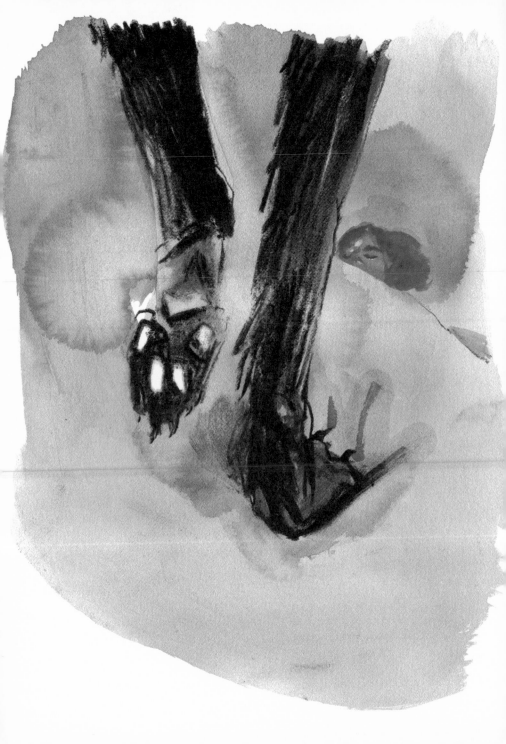

# GOOD BOY

Sweating.  A scream climbing up through her chest.

*Your heels at the edge of the drop.  The bright worms way, way down there.*

She reaches for Rabbie.  Her hand knocks over a glass of water.

*And now it's nearer than ever before and you see the moon madness in its eyes and its lips drawn back from its teeth and the rippled roof of its mouth and its slobber and it launches itself at you, its body all muscle and hot stink—*

Screaming.

"Good boy!  Good boy!"

She gropes, fingers finding only wet carpet.
She sits up.  Her hand clatters the bedside
table, finds the light switch.  The shock of being
in the familiar room.

The terror fades into the light, but it's like
it's never been gone.

\*

Nor does it leave her now.  It haunts her days
as well as her nights.  Shadows of its shape slip
down corridors, alleyways.  She glimpses its

reflection in shop windows. It emerges from

innocent hedges and sits, tensed, waiting for

her to come closer before it disappears.

## 8

As when she was a child, Sandie starts avoiding sleep. It affects her work. She is tired, she forgets things. After a few months, her boss suggests she see a therapist.

This one is not at all like Aziza. He is bald but has a small beard. It's like his hair has slid down his head and gathered at his chin ready to fall into his lap. His name is Mark.

She tells him about the dog that haunts her life.

"What do you do for a living, Sandie? Is it OK if I call you Sandie?"

"Sure," she says. "I'm a police officer."

"Really. Like, a detective?"

"No. An ordinary copper."

"Hmm. That can be a dangerous job, can't it? Especially in this city. So would you describe yourself as a brave person? A confident person?"

"I used to be," Sandie says.

Mark nods and picks up a pen. "So tell me what frightens you. Apart from the nightmare dog, of course."

"The usual things," she says. "Spiders. Nutters with axes in their hands, cancer, heights ..."

He interrupts. "Not everyone is scared of heights, actually. Mountaineers, for instance. Scaffolders."

She shrugs. "I guess."

After a pause, Mark says, "The black dog is sometimes a metaphor for depression. Do you think you're depressed, Sandie?"

"No."

All the same, Mark describes the symptoms
of depression.  Sandie has to agree that
some of them match her own.  Mark writes
her a prescription and arranges another
appointment in a month's time.

Two weeks later, Sandie flushes the tablets
down the toilet.  She skips the appointment.

\*

The dog continues to haunt her.

# 9

On a November night, with the sky a dark
blank above the sullen yellow street lights,
Sandie Callan is in a patrol car with her regular
partner and driver, PC Simon "Wheelie" Binns.
They're thinking about picking up a couple of
coffees when Control comes on the radio.

"Oscar Papa three-zero," Sandie says into
the mike. "Go ahead."

# GOOD BOY

"Reported violent incident at Dover House on the Eden estate."

"Well, fancy that," Wheelie murmurs, swinging the car left to make a U-turn.

"Probably a domestic," Control says, "but watch yourself. Whisky Bravo also alerted."

"Wilco," Sandie says.

Wheelie turns on the flashers and the siren. Accelerates. The street lights race backwards like a madman's blinking.

*

Like the other three buildings on the Eden estate, Dover House is a huge slab of a place jutting rudely up into the sky. Walkways run along each of its ten levels. *It's the kind of place*, Sandie thinks, *you'd only live in if life had dealt you a very bad hand.*

# GOOD BOY

When they get out of the car, there are people waiting for them; they back off and stand watching like humans witnessing the arrival of an alien spacecraft. But there is screaming and shouting from up the face of the building. Silhouettes against the broken and flickering light along the walkways, pointing in various directions.

Sandie and Wheelie stand, staring up, uncertain. Then a man in dreadlocks, an older man, says from behind them, "It's kickin' off on level six, man. But I wouldn' go up there if I was you."

Wheelie says, "What d'you think?"

"Call back-up," Sandie says.

Wheelie reaches back into the car and talks into the radio.

Then there's two pops like cheap fireworks and a chorus of screams.

"C'mon," Sandie shouts, already running towards the entry.

"No!" Wheelie yells, but she's gone.

# 10

At ground level there's nobody, just a long

line of bin bags sitting like black toads, some

of them spilling their guts. At the end of the

corridor there are two sets of lift doors. Sandie

whacks her palm against both sets of buttons

but, as she expected, nothing happens. She

sets off up the stairs. By the time she gets

to six, her lungs feel as though they're full of

broken glass. She leans against the wall of the

stairwell, dragging in air, then risks a peek

around the corner of the walkway.  There's

a young guy, a boy, sitting on the concrete

ten metres away.  His mouth is open, but he's

making no sound.  His hands are clutched at

his stomach, but they're not stopping the blood

leaking onto his lap.  Just beyond him a girl is

crawling slowly away. In the hard overhead

light the trail of blood she's making shines

black. There's no one else. All the doors along

the walkway are shut.

Wheelie is yelling in Sandie's earpiece. She

ignores him and switches her collar-mike to

*send* and jabbers the codes for Ambulance and

Armed Response Units.  For whatever reason,
she thinks she must stop the girl crawling.  The
boy gazes at her as she passes him; shock has
frozen his face in a smile.  Sandie gets in front
of the girl and kneels and puts her hands on
the girl's shoulders.

"It's OK," Sandie says, but then the girl
falls onto her side and Sandie knows it isn't.
The hoodie and the mini and the tights are
drenched dark red.

There's a sound from the stairs end of
the walkway, and Sandie looks up.  Her hand
reaches for her taser, but it's Wheelie.  She's

surprised he got up here so fast; he's not the fittest man at the station.  He's bent over, his hands on his knees.

"Callan," he gasps.  "Callan, you …"

Then he takes in the scene.

"Dear God."

Sandie pushes past him.

"Do what you can for them," she says.  "The shooter went up, or we'd've met him on the stairs."

"Sandie, no."

But she's gone.

# GOOD BOY

Climbing the last four flights, fear and exhaustion thud her heart. At the tenth floor, as before, she peers round the corner. No one. Behind and to the right of her there's an unmarked door. She risks pushing it. It opens. Nothing terrible happens. Behind the door there's a space not much bigger than a cupboard. Two of the walls have thick power cables running down them. On the third there's a metal ladder. She climbs it and feels the cold breath of night on her face. Then, as she'd feared, she finds herself on the roof.

# 11

It's a flat area more or less the size of a football pitch. Towards one end there's a metal thicket of telecom aerials. Running down its centre there are four low structures a bit like sheds with slatted walls. The surface is black and puddled and gritty underfoot. Sandie walks cautiously to the far side of the roof to the fire escapes. As far as she can see, there's nobody on them. Far below, the lights of traffic are

# GOOD BOY

twisting worms of red and white and yellow.

And blue, flickering.  The moan of approaching

patrol cars swells, fades, swells again.

 The roof of Folkestone House is level with

her, and close.  You could almost jump the gap.

But not quite.  The thought makes her feel sick.

MAL PEET

She retreats from the edge of the precipice.

She should not be up here.  The jabbering

in her earpiece is telling her that.  She is,

suddenly, both sensible and afraid.

She heads back towards the roof access, but

before she can reach it a hooded human shape

steps out from behind one of the shed-like

things.  He's holding a gun in both hands.  Light

from somewhere makes a blue line down its

barrel.  He giggles.

It's the giggle that chills Sandie to the core.

She knows that a man who giggles when he's

aiming a gun at you is not the kind of man you can reason with.

All the same, she tries. She spreads her arms away from her body.

"I'm unarmed. Put the gun down. Please don't be stupid. You've got nowhere to go."

Wrong thing to say.

He takes a step towards her. All she can see of his face is the tip of his nose and then a flicker of tongue as he licks his lips.

"Yeah," he says. "I got nowhere to go."

He laughs like he's choking.

# GOOD BOY

"I'm going nowhere. I fink I might take you wiv me."

Sandie turns her head and measures the distance to the fire escapes.

*It's worth a try*, she thinks, then her heart seems to stop its mad beating. She stops breathing because the black dog is stalking along the parapet of Folkestone House like a ripple in the dull sky. Its ears are alert triangles. Its eyes are two orange flames, watching her. She can see the flesh bunching in its shoulders and haunches. It lifts its upper lip in something like a smile. Sandie hears the

long low growl deep in its throat: a sound like

bubbling blood.

She understands.

The dog is death.  Her death.

Sandie hears the metallic click of the gun

behind her.

She gets ready to die.  The only words in

her head are, for some reason, *I'm so sorry,*

*Mum.*

Then the beast leaps.  Flies towards

her across the dizzying space between the

buildings.  Its shape seems to fill the sky,

blacking it out.

Sandie falls onto her knees.  She raises

her arms, perhaps in a hopeless attempt to

protect herself from the animal.  Or perhaps to

welcome it.  She closes her eyes.

A long inhuman scream splits the night.

MAL PEET

It's not Sandie's scream.  It's not her agony.

She turns.  The dog has the gunman down

on his back, tearing at him, its thick whip of

a tail thrashing.  Dog and man are a single

writhing shape, howling and snarling.  Then

the man's right arm emerges.  The hand has

the gun in it still.  He shoots the dog, twice,

up through its body.  Sandie clearly sees the

pouts in the dog's back where the bullets exit.

But no sprays of blood.  And the creature is

unaffected; if anything, the shots only increase

its savagery.  It twists its massive shoulders

and seizes the man's wrist with its jaws,

jerking it as if it were breaking the neck of a

rat. Sandie hears, or imagines, the fracturing

of bones, the parting of sinews. The gun

skitters across the roof and comes to rest in a

puddle. The dog releases the man's arm and

stands over him, panting, as though making

a decision. Then it attacks again, going for

face and throat. The man's feet pedal the air

helplessly.

## 12

Sandie walks unsteadily towards her nightmare.
She stands above the struggle, uncertain. Then
she puts her hand on the back of the dog's neck,
feeling the soft roll of fat and muscle beneath
its hot fur. Squeezes it gently.

"Good boy," she says. "Good boy."

Its head comes up, the hot eyes rolling, the
murderous mouth gaping.

Although she is very afraid, she runs her
hand softly down to its shoulders.

"Good boy."

Its body relaxes. It steps away from the
man, who is now twisting and moaning like
someone disturbed in his sleep. Sandie looks
down at him, expecting to see rips, wounds.
There are none.

The dog sits beside her, panting, its red
tongue steaming.

The night fills with a heavy throbbing. For
a moment Sandie thinks it is the hammering
of her heart. Then a helicopter slides sideways

into the sky and drenches the roof in harsh

light.

A hugely amplified voice speaks to her from

above; she cannot make out the words.  At the

same instant, four armed officers burst onto

the roof.

One of them thinks he sees a dark shape

poised on the parapet as if about to leap.  He

aims his weapon, but there's nothing.

The only persons on the roof are

Sandie Callan and, just a few paces from

her, a man sitting with his face in his

hands, shaking and sobbing like someone

waking from a nightmare.